P9-DGG-121

Days of the Ducklings

written and photo-illustrated by

Bruce McMillan

Houghton Mifflin Company Boston 2001

Walter Lorraine Books

Tileinkuð Friðrik Jónssyni, sem elskar börn sín og eyjar

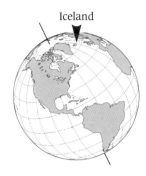

Iceland

Days of the Ducklings was made possible through the help and assistance of
my newfound friend and the book's photographic subject, Drífa Friðriksdóttir;
her older brother and sister, Jón Örn Friðriksson and Erla Friðriksdóttir;
the six island owners and advisors, Friðrik Jónsson (Drífa's father),
Þorvaldur Þór Björnsson, Guðmundur Þorbjörn Björnsson,
Andrés Bjarnason, Kristján Þórðarson, and Guðjón Egilsson;
the island cooks, Hjördis Jónsdóttir and Sigriour Pálsdóttir;
Kristján Egilsson, director of the Museum of
Natural History and Aquarium in Vestmannaeyjar;
Einar Gùstavsson, the Icelandic Tourist Board;
and Maria Mitchell and Debbie Scott, Media Relations, Icelandair.

The photographs were taken during the summer of 1999 on Hvallátur Island, Iceland,
using a Nikon F4/MF23 with 24, 85, 105 micro, 180, 300, and 600 millimeter lenses.
A polarizing filter was often used when shooting in full sunlight.
The 35 millimeter film, Kodachrome 64, was processed by Kodak at Fair Lawn, New Jersey.
Insulated chest-high waders enabled shooting in the cold ocean water with the ducklings.

More information can be found at www.brucemcmillan.com.

Walter Lorraine 🎨 Books
Copyright © 2001 by Bruce McMillan

Library of Congress Cataloging-in-Publication Data
McMillan, Bruce.
Days of the Ducklings / written and photo-illustrated by Bruce McMillan
p. c.m.
Includes bibliographical references.
ISBN 0-618-04878-2 (hardcover)
1. Eider — Iceland — Hvallátur Island — Juvenile literature.
2. Eider — Iceland — Hvallátur Island — Pictorial works — Juvenile literature.
[1. Eider. 2. Ducks.] I. Title.
QL696.A52   M39   2001
598.4'15 — dc21
00-013258

Printed in Singapore
TWP 10 9 8 7 6 5 4 3 2 1

Designed by Bruce McMillan
The text is set in 14-point Caxton

Seventy-five miles (one hundred and twenty kilometers) south of the Arctic Circle

Hvallátur *(kvah · LAHW · ter)* Island, Iceland
June

   "Arr-ROOO. Arr-ROOO." The sounds of eider ducks
fill the air. Black-and-white males paddle nearby.
Camouflage-patterned brown females come ashore to nest
on nearby islands.
   Now, only a few nest on the island of Hvallátur.
Drífa *(DREE · vah)* has come to change that.

Not as many eiders have come here since Hvallátur was used for farming, abandoned, and then sold. To help the ducks return, the new owners cleared away leftover debris. Then the Icelandic government granted them permission to raise and release wild ducklings. Drífa, whose father is an owner, has come from Reykjavík *(RAYK·yah·veek)* to put their plan into action.

On a nearby island, she gathers eggs and collects fluffy down feathers. The down will be cleaned and sold to fill jackets and blankets.

In one nest she finds five eggs. She replaces the down with straw to keep the eggs warm. The mother eider scurries back to her nest and settles on her eggs. She doesn't notice that Drífa has taken one.

Drífa visits a number of nearby islands. She gathers more than two hundred eggs, one by one, over many days. On Hvallátur, Drífa keeps the eggs warm. She watches closely as each duckling pecks through its shell.

The hatchlings huddle under the protection of their caregiver. When a new one joins the group, Drífa whispers to herself, "Æðarungi" *(EYE·thar·ung·gee)*, which means "eider duckling" in Icelandic.

Drífa's work has just begun.

10

When the ducklings aren't sleeping, they eat, drink, and leave droppings. Day after day Drífa sets out food, fills their watering stations, and scrapes up their droppings.

The young ducklings peep rapidly when they are excited. When Drífa leads them outside, the ducklings *"peep-peep-peep"* as fast as they can.

The ducklings group together, as they would in the wild. When Drífa lies down to nap, the ducklings nap, too. They cluster all over her.

She knows they are content. She listens to the happy sounds of their breathing trills. They are so appealing. Drífa knows it would be easy to forget that if they are to survive later in the wild she cannot think of them as pets.

Drífa knows they are really wild birds. She does not allow
herself to hold them, even though she wants to.

She calls *"buk-buk-buk,"* and they answer her with their
"cah-cah-cah-coooo." It's time to show them more of the
island. The ducklings follow Drífa to the water's edge.

Into the water they go, the oldest duckling leading the way, splashing, bobbing, and exploring. They can't go far because the tide is out, leaving the ducklings their own shallow pool warmed by the sun.

Drífa watches over them. She also watches the sky. Gulls often attack the defenseless ducklings. If she needs to, she will chase away any black-backed seagulls, but fortunately on this day none appear.

The ducklings swim the way they walk, first one foot forward and then the other. Their webbed feet push them through the water. They dive below the surface of the water and peck at the bottom. Instinct guides them.

Before the tide comes in—and before they get too cold— Drífa calls *"buk-buk-buk."* The ducklings come running. Some of them stray but finally find their way back.

As much as she wants to, Drífa resists patting them. Though she loves each and every duckling, she can't let them become too attached to her.

She has also resisted picking up and carrying strays during their daily trips to the cove. Instead, she builds a walkway to help them find their own way.

After Drífa is finished building, the ducklings awake.
They fluff their feathers. Drífa calls *"poh-poh-poh-poh-poh."*
The ducklings discover that the pen is open. The walkway
works.

As the young eiders grow, they come and go on their own.
They could go farther out in the water but they don't. They
stay together, where it's familiar. They poke around in the
water, learning to eat small shellfish and crustaceans.

The ducklings stretch their new young wings. Next summer their full-grown wings will carry them around the islands at speeds as fast as fifty miles per hour.

But this summer they must walk back to the area where Drífa has set food out for them. Drífa gives them more food than ducklings in the wild would have, so they are slightly larger. Now a month old, some of Drífa's ducklings have almost tripled in weight to six ounces (one hundred and seventy grams).

By July the eider ducklings are spending more time in the water. No longer are they snuggling up to Drífa. But as she watches over them, they still gather near her. Murmuring their low-throated *"cah-cah-cah-coooo,"* they still talk to her. Drífa knows this too must change.

Soon, it does. Now, Drífa watches from afar. The ducklings go farther and farther from her, searching for food. No longer do they return to the grassy pen. No longer do they follow Drífa. Now they follow their instincts.

Drífa is both happy and sad. Her work is done. They are wild eider ducks. They are exploring their new home. They will survive.

29

By early August it's time for Drífa to leave, to return to her home on the mainland. It's time for the young eiders to face the world in their own way.

Hopefully these eiders will spend the winter here. Hopefully they will stay and make Hvallátur Island their home. Hopefully they will be here when Drífa returns next summer.

31

Male eider duck
Icelandic: Bliki *(BLEEK · ee)*

Eider duckling
Icelandic: Æðarungi *(EYE · thar · ung · gee)*

Female eider duck
Icelandic: Kolla *(KOT · lar)*

Common Eider Ducks *(Somateria mollissima)*

The common eider is the largest duck in the Northern Hemisphere. Although eiders may be hunted in North America, they cannot be hunted in Iceland. Since 1847 the common eider has been a protected species. Here they are treasured for their unique down.

When a female nests, she plucks and sheds down feathers from her belly. This leaves her warm skin in contact with the eggs. It also surrounds and insulates her eggs with fluffy down feathers. The temperature in a nest can be up to 99.5 degrees Fahrenheit (37.5 degrees centigrade), even if the surrounding temperature is only 36 degrees Fahrenheit (3 degrees centigrade). Eider down is one of the lightest and most effective insulators. It's collected without harming the eggs and replaced with straw. It's harvested and used in jackets, sleeping bags, and comforters. A down feather is literally "as light as a feather." It takes about 13,500 hand-picked feathers to make one ounce (twenty-eight grams).

The west coast of Iceland is a major breeding area for common eiders. At the center of this area, in the bay of Breiðafjörður *(BRAY · tha · fyor · thur),* lies the Hvallátur chain of about two hundred and forty islands. Icelanders first arrived at Hvallátur in the 1200s. More recently the home island has been used as a farm. However, after it was abandoned, a collective of owners, including Drifa's father, purchased and cleaned up this island to restore it to its natural state. They also procured a license from the Icelandic Ministry for the Environment to raise eiders.

In the summer of 1999, when this book was photographed, Drífa and others gathered two hundred and eight eggs from other islands in the Hvallátur chain. It was Drífa's responsibility to care for them and raise the young eiders. She kept meticulous records. One of the island's owners banded each duckling's leg with a lightweight aluminum band imprinted with an identifying number. At summer's end all but seven ducklings, which were lost to disease and accidents, were swimming around the island.

Selected Bibliography

Bárðarson, Hjálmar R. *Birds of Iceland*. Reykjavík: Bárðarson, 1986.

Björnsson, A., Gíslason, E.G., and Petersen, Æ. *Ferðafélag Íslands Árbók 1989, Breiðafjarðareyjar*. Reykjavík: Ferðafélag Íslands, 1989.

Einarsson, Þorsteinn. *Guide to the Birds of Iceland*. Reykjavík: Örn og Örlygur Publishing House, 1991.

Rand, Austin L. *Ornithology, an Introduction*. New York: Norton, 1967.

"Ungviði í Öndvegi í Hvallátrum," *Morgunbaðið*. 28 June 1998, Sunday edition, pages B1, B8, and B9.

Eider down close-up